HIDE!
The tiger's mouth is open wide!

By Adam Frost

Stop! There's a Snake in Your Suitcase!
Run! The Elephant Weighs a Ton!
Catch that Bat!
Hide! The Tiger's Mouth is Open Wide!

HIDE!

The tiger's mouth is open wide!

Adam Frost

Illustrated by
Mark Chambers

BLOOMSBURY
LONDON NEW DELHI NEW YORK SYDNEY

All of the animal facts in this story are true.
Everything else is fiction. Any connection
to any events that have taken place in
London Zoo is purely coincidental.

Bloomsbury Publishing, London, New Delhi, New York and Sydney

First published in Great Britain in July 2013 by Bloomsbury Publishing Plc
50 Bedford Square, London WC1B 3DP

Manufactured and supplied under licence from the Zoological Society of London

A CIP catalogue record for this book is available from the British Library

ISBN 978 1 4088 2709 3

Typeset by Hewer Text UK Ltd, Edinburgh
Printed and bound in Great Britain by CPI Group (UK) Ltd, Croydon CR0 4YY

3 5 7 9 10 8 6 4 2

www.storiesfromthezoo.com
www.bloomsbury.com
www.adam-frost.com

To Molly and Joel

Chapter 1

'Tom! Where are you?' shouted Mrs Nightingale.

But her son was nowhere to be found.

First she looked around the houseboat where they lived. She checked all three bedrooms, the living room, the kitchen, the bathroom, the deck and the roof.

Then she walked out on the towpath where the houseboat was moored. She looked up and down the canal bank and shouted 'Tom!' again.

She walked down to her father's boat. His barge, the *Molly Magee*, was moored fifty metres further down the towpath. She swung herself on to the deck and opened the door.

1

'Is Tom in here, Dad?' she asked.

Grandad was watching a cricket match on the television. His feet were in a washing-up bowl full of hot water.

''Fraid not, Katie,' Grandad replied. 'You're OUT, sir!' he shouted at the television.

Mrs Nightingale walked back along the canal, peering into all the bushes and glancing up at the trees, checking to see if Tom was in any of his usual hiding places.

She climbed back on to *The Ark*, which was the nickname of their boat. It had potted

plants on the roof and wild animals painted on both sides.

Her daughter, Sophie, was sitting by the kitchen table, wearing her coat and gloves.

'Sophie, do you know where your brother is?' Mrs Nightingale asked. 'We can't leave without him.'

Sophie got up with a sigh. 'This happens every time. Can't you just tell him we're going to the zoo instead?'

'Lying is wrong, Sophie,' Mrs Nightingale said. 'Besides, I tried that last time and he saw right through it.'

Tom was hiding. He had made up his mind about half an hour earlier and had tiptoed through the living room and off the houseboat. His mother and sister were too busy to notice – they were talking about a new ocelot that had arrived at London Zoo, where Mrs Nightingale worked as Chief Vet.

As he closed the front door, one of the family

cats – Mindy – slid outside too and curled herself around Tom's legs.

'Can't stroke you now, Mindy,' Tom said. 'Got to hide.'

He ran along the towpath and climbed up the bank towards the wall that separated the canal from the street. Then he walked along the wall for about ten metres, wobbling and veering from one side to the other, before lowering himself down off the end. He was now in the field behind the London Zoo car park, creeping through the long grass. When he reached an iron gate, he vaulted over, landing in the local boat repair yard. This was where barges were taken out of the water to be fixed or repainted or resealed. A small red houseboat was currently in the dry dock, propped up on wooden trestles, with half its hull missing.

Tom spotted what he'd been looking for – the foreman's shed. He quickly slid behind it, and sat down next to a tree. He was completely out of sight. He got his portable games console out of his pocket and started to play Ninja Hippos.

Five minutes later, Sophie stuck her head behind the shed. 'Come on, Tom,' she said. 'Time to go.'

So Mrs Nightingale, Tom and Sophie all went to the dentist's together.

Tom couldn't believe that Sophie had found him so quickly. She must have heard the beeps and pings from his games console. Next time, he'd turn the sound right down or bring his headphones.

'Honestly, Tom, the dentist isn't that bad,' said Mrs Nightingale. 'You don't want to end up with brown teeth like Great-Uncle Humphrey, do you?'

'Mm-nnn-mmm,' said Tom, keeping his lips clamped tightly together.

'It only takes about half an hour,' said Mrs Nightingale, 'and then it's over for another six months.'

'Nn-mm-nnn,' said Tom, still keeping his mouth firmly closed.

'What on earth are you doing?' Mrs Nightingale said. 'I can't understand a word you're saying.'

'I think he's refusing to open his mouth,' said Sophie. 'That way, the dentist can't look at his teeth.'

Tom pointed at Sophie and nodded. Then he pointed at his jaw.

'It's because they gave him a filling last time,' said Sophie.

Tom said, 'Mm-nn,' and pointed at Sophie again.

'Well, if you spent more than three seconds brushing your teeth, you wouldn't need any fillings,' said Mrs Nightingale.

When they arrived at the dentist's, they sat down in the waiting room, side by side. Tom was still refusing to open his mouth.

Sophie tickled him under the ribs and he burst out laughing, but still managed to keep his mouth closed, laughing with his eyes and snorting through his nose while fending her off with his arm.

'Mm-nn!' he said angrily, when he'd stopped laughing.

Dr Sharp, the dentist, appeared in the door-way. He had wavy brown hair and a big beard.

'Hello, Tom. Hello, Sophie. Who wants to go first?'

Tom folded his arms and looked the other way.

'Tom it is,' said Dr Sharp. 'Come on through.'

Tom shook his head.

'Come on, Tom, there's nothing to worry about,' the dentist said with a smile.

Tom shook his head again and clenched his jaw more tightly than ever. Then he clamped his hand to his mouth.

'Let me tell you something,' Dr Sharp said. He leant forward and whispered something in Tom's ear.

Tom's eyebrows shot up. He got up and walked quietly across the waiting room and into Dr Sharp's surgery.

Sophie and Mrs Nightingale looked at each other in disbelief.

They remained puzzled for another ten minutes, after which time Tom reappeared in the waiting room with a gleaming smile.

'So what happened?' Mrs Nightingale asked.

'Yeah, why do you look so happy?' Sophie asked. 'Did you get a badge or something?'

'What? Oh, er, no,' Tom said. 'Actually, you won't believe this – Dr Sharp said if I let him look at my teeth, I could go and help him next week.'

'What are you talking about?' Sophie asked.

'Ohhhh, I see,' said Mrs Nightingale.

'Can someone tell me what's going on?' Sophie asked.

Dr Sharp appeared behind Tom. 'Your turn, Sophie.'

'OK, but only if you tell me how you managed to get Tom in your dentist's chair,' Sophie said.

Dr Sharp grinned. 'Oh, it was simple enough. You see, as well as looking at human teeth, I also inspect the animals in London Zoo once a year. They need a check-up once in a while, just like you. And next Sunday is my official visiting day. I said to Tom that if he let me look at his teeth, then he could come with me on my rounds.'

'Oh . . . OK . . .' Sophie stammered.

'You're included in that offer too,' Dr Sharp said.

'Amazing, right?' Tom said.

Sophie nodded, too dumbstruck to answer.

'I can't believe I didn't want to come to the dentist,' said Tom. 'It's brilliant here. And it doesn't hurt at all. Honestly, Sophie, there's nothing to worry about.'

'I *know* that,' said Sophie.

'Cool,' said Tom airily, and sat back down in his chair. Then he picked up a comic that was lying on the table next to him and started to read it.

'You're unbelievable, you know that,' said Sophie.

Tom smiled. 'Thanks, Soph.'

Chapter 2

The following Sunday, Tom and Sophie were racing each other to the zoo. They always went to the zoo at least once at the weekend because both their parents worked there – their dad as a zookeeper and their mum as Chief Vet.

Today was a Big Day though. Dr Sharp was going to meet them at the gates.

'Do you think he'll examine *all* the animals?' Tom asked as they trotted across the bridge that led to the zoo.

'I suppose he'll have to,' said Sophie.

'But they've got, like, fifteen thousand different ones,' Tom said.

'It's more like seventeen thousand,' said Sophie, 'so yeah, maybe he'll just look at the ones with sore teeth.'

'And I suppose not all the animals have teeth,' Tom said. 'I mean worms don't have teeth, do they? Or budgies? Or goldfish?'

'I don't know,' said Sophie.

'Or spiders? Or frogs?' Tom continued.

'I'm not sure,' said Sophie.

'And some animals have massive teeth, don't they?' said Tom. 'It would take him ages to look at an elephant's tusks. And what about a walrus's. Or a warthog's!'

'Yeah, and the zoo's got five warthogs,' said Sophie, 'and they've each got two pairs of tusks. That's . . . twenty warthog tusks!'

When they reached the zoo gates, Dr Sharp was waiting for them. Next to him was a friendly-looking young woman with spiky purple hair and bright red lipstick.

'This is Violet,' said Dr Sharp. 'She's my assistant.'

'Hi, Tom! Hi, Sophie!' Violet greeted them enthusiastically. 'Dr Sharp has told me that you're London Zoo experts.'

'I don't know about that . . .' Sophie said.

'That's right!' exclaimed Tom. 'Ask us anything you like!'

'OK,' Violet said with a smile. 'Where can I get a massive chocolate croissant for my breakfast?'

Tom and Sophie smiled. 'This way!' Tom said, and led the way to the Oasis cafe.

After Violet had bought her croissant, Dr Sharp took an electronic notebook out of a black case that he was holding. He glanced at it quickly and said, 'First up is Colin the camel. He's a Bactrian camel, so he'll have two humps. Bactrians originally come from the Gobi Desert in east Asia, but where does he live now?'

'Over here!' said Tom.

'You've got to be careful with Colin,' said Sophie, as they walked across the picnic lawn. 'He's got a bit of a temper.'

'Make sure he doesn't bite you,' said Tom. 'His teeth are like daggers.'

'Well, his canine teeth will be like daggers,' said Violet. 'They're these teeth here. The ones like Dracula's fangs.'

She pointed to the two pointy teeth in her own mouth.

'But as for the rest of his teeth,' Violet went on, 'they won't be like daggers at all. They'll be pretty flat.'

'What do you mean?' Tom asked.

'Well, camels are herbivores,' said Violet. 'That means they only eat plants. Which tends to involve lots of chewing. Camels grind down grass and leaves and vegetables for hours and hours every day. For that, they need lots of rounded flat teeth.'

'So it's only carnivores that need sharp teeth?' said Sophie.

'As a rule, yes.' said Violet. 'If you're a meat-eater, you need strong, pointed teeth to kill your prey and tear the flesh off their bodies.'

Tom smiled. 'Cool.'

'Of course, there are also omnivores,' said Dr Sharp.

'What do they eat? Omelettes?' Tom asked.

'They eat everything!' Violet said. 'We're omnivores. That's why we have sharp teeth at the front and flat teeth at the back.'

'It means we can gnaw a chicken drumstick *and* chew on a salad,' said Dr Sharp.

They had arrived at the camels' enclosure. Mr and Mrs Nightingale were waiting for them.

'Roger, Violet, good to see you,' said Mrs Nightingale.

'So what's up with Colin?' Dr Sharp asked.

'Nothing really. He just needs a check-up,' said Mr Nightingale.

'OK, let's have a look at him,' said Dr Sharp.

They all went inside the enclosure and Colin ambled over. Mr Nightingale gave the command 'Kush!' and Colin lowered himself down on to the floor. His legs completely vanished underneath his large brown shaggy body.

Then Mr Nightingale put his arm around Colin's neck and started to whisper to him. 'OK, we're just going to look inside your mouth. No need to panic.'

Dr Sharp gently lifted up Colin's lips. Colin shied away, but Mr Nightingale held his neck more tightly and stopped him rearing back.

'A camel's mouth and teeth are perfectly adapted to their native environment,' Violet said to Tom and Sophie, as Dr Sharp poked around in Colin's mouth.

'You mean life in the desert?' Sophie asked.

'Exactly,' said Violet. 'He's got a split lip, which lets him grip on to tough desert plants and strip leaves from spiky branches. The skin on his lips is tough too, so all those prickly cactuses and thorny twigs don't hurt his mouth at all.'

'So if I had teeth like that, then could I survive in the desert?' said Tom, feeling his own mouth.

'His teeth have to be strong too,' said Violet,

'to tear those plants out of the ground, and then to chew them up.'

Tom looked again at Dr Sharp who was now prodding Colin's gums gently. Colin was getting restless again.

'Does Dr Sharp like his fingers?' Tom asked.

'Let me stroke Colin, Dad,' Sophie said. 'He's always liked me.'

Mr Nightingale nodded and moved to one side; Sophie came close and started to stroke the fur on Colin's back.

'Excellent, all done,' said Dr Sharp. 'He just needs a quick scrub now.'

He reached down into his case and pulled out a gigantic toothbrush. It was more like a back scrubber or a toilet brush.

'OK, this is when Colin might kick off,' Mr Nightingale said. 'Are you sure you're OK there, Sophie?'

'We're fine,' Sophie said, continuing to hug Colin's neck.

Dr Sharp squirted some toothpaste on to

the brush. Tom expected the toothpaste to be in a giant tube too, but it was actually normal-sized. Then Dr Sharp started to scrub Colin's front teeth. Colin, flinched, pulling his neck backwards as he began to push up with his front feet. Sophie slid off the camel's neck and landed on the hard floor of the enclosure with a jolt. Dr Sharp dropped his toothbrush and Mrs Nightingale instinctively pushed Tom behind her.

Mr Nightingale reached down for the harness that he had clipped to his belt. But Sophie was back on her feet, gently stroking Colin again.

Colin leaned towards Sophie, lifting his neck up and staring ahead with a calm expression. Sophie gently put pressure on Colin's neck, urging him to sit back down.

'Let's go down together,' she said quietly.

At first Colin's legs stiffened and he seemed to refuse but, as Sophie kept stroking and whispering, his legs slowly gave way and he lowered himself back down.

'Good work, Sophie,' Mr Nightingale said.

Dr Sharp picked up the toothbrush again.

'Shall I have another try?' he asked.

Colin seemed to understand the question and immediately hissed at the dentist.

'Colin likes Tom too,' Sophie suggested. 'Maybe if Tom was doing the brushing, Colin wouldn't mind so much.'

Dr Sharp looked down at Tom and nodded. 'OK with me, if it's OK with Tom.'

Tom was handed the giant toothbrush. He stared at it as if it was a sword, not really knowing what to do with it.

'Go for it, Tom,' Violet said.

Tom snapped out of his trance and nodded. He looked up at Colin and took a couple of steps forward. When he was close enough, he gently put the toothbrush in the camel's mouth.

Tom started to brush hesitantly, but then got more confident, scrubbing away at Colin's front teeth, which were yellow and crusted with gunk. Sophie continued to stroke Colin's fur and hum soothing songs.

'OK, that's fine,' said Dr Sharp after a few minutes.

'Oh,' Tom moaned. 'I only just started.'

'He has the cleanest teeth in London,' said Violet. 'Zoo visitors will have to wear sunglasses to protect themselves from the glare.'

Tom handed back the toothbrush reluctantly. 'What about floss?' he asked, looking suddenly hopeful.

'He doesn't need floss,' Dr Sharp said.

'Mouthwash?'

Dr Sharp and Violet shook their heads.

'You were very helpful though,' Dr Sharp said. 'I don't think Colin likes me at all. Fancy helping me with our next patient?'

'Who's next?' Sophie asked.

'Harriet the pygmy hippo,' said Dr Sharp.

'Definitely!' Tom and Sophie said together.

* ★ ★

A few minutes later, Mrs Nightingale was leading Dr Sharp, Violet, Tom and Sophie into the hippos' enclosure. Mr Nightingale had gone on ahead to lure Harriet out of her pool.

'Are hippos herbivores or carnivores?' Tom asked.

'Herbivores,' said Dr Sharp.

'So they're peaceful, plant-eating creatures then,' said Tom.

'Not exactly,' said Violet.

'Not exactly?' Sophie asked.

'OK, I mean not at all,' said Violet. 'Yes, hippos eat plants, so they have lots of flat molars at the back of their mouths to grind and chew vegetable matter. But they also have to defend themselves against lions, crocodiles and sometimes other hippos. So they have some of the longest, sharpest canine teeth of any land animal. And their teeth are the hardest in the world – some people think they can even deflect bullets!'

'Wow!' exclaimed Tom.

'You've seen a photo of a hippo with its mouth open?' Dr Sharp asked.

Tom and Sophie nodded.

'If it chooses to clamp it shut, it can kill a lion with a single bite.'

Sophie bit her bottom lip and looked at Tom, who had a slightly worried expression on his face.

'And you're going to put your head in its mouth?' Tom asked.

'Hang on,' Dr Sharp said. 'First of all, we're not lions or a crocodiles. And secondly, she's a pygmy hippo, so everything's a lot smaller, including her teeth.'

Tom and Sophie felt slightly calmer until they turned a corner and saw Harriet, standing by the edge of her pool, with her mouth wide open and her large canine teeth shining in the sun.

'Whoa,' they both said, taking two steps backwards.

Mr Nightingale appeared and looked

confused. 'No need to worry, kids,' he said. 'I'm just getting her ready for Dr Sharp. We've trained her to open her mouth.' He held up the whistle around his neck.

Tom and Sophie relaxed slightly.

Harriet was about one metre tall and almost two metres long, with a slighty rounder head than a full-sized hippo.

Mr Nightingale pointed to a red mark on Harriet's top lip. He said, 'I first noticed this about a month ago and it's got steadily worse.

I don't think it's a cut or a sore, so I'm a bit at a loss as to what's causing it.'

Dr Sharp and Violet poked gently around in Harriet's mouth. Harriet's eyes shifted uneasily but she kept her mouth open.

'She's very patient, isn't she?' Sophie said.

'She's a patient patient,' said Tom with a grin. 'Geddit?'

'Hilarious,' said Sophie.

Dr Sharp finished examining Harriet and turned to face everyone. 'Her teeth are to blame for her sore lip. See her lower right canine, here?' He pointed at one of the long sharp teeth in the hippo's bottom jaw. 'It's got slightly wonky and started to dig into her lip every time she closes her mouth.'

Mr Nightingale nodded. 'So what do we do?' he asked.

Violet bent down and pulled a giant nail file out of her bag.

'Wow, is any of your equipment normal-sized?' Tom asked.

'Every morning you need to file the side of her tooth down with this. To make it straighter. Starting this morning.'

'Won't that hurt her?' said Sophie.

Violet shook her head. 'There are no nerves in the outer ivory of her teeth. It will tickle her slightly, but it won't hurt.'

'I'm great at filing!' Tom said. 'I helped Dad make a coffee table for our houseboat. I had to make all the edges smooth. So if you need a hand . . .'

'I think your Dad should probably go first,' Violet said. 'It's pretty tough going. Remember, her teeth are among the strongest in the world.'

'OK,' said Tom begrudgingly.

Mr Nightingale started to file down the side of Harriet's wonky tooth. When he'd removed some of the ivory, he handed the file back to Violet.

'Can I have a go now?' asked Tom.

'And me too!' said Sophie.

'Well, I suppose there's no harm in you having a try,' said Violet.

'Me first!' said Tom, and Sophie rolled her eyes, as Violet passed Tom the file.

The file was so heavy and the tooth so tough that they didn't make much progress.

'Never mind,' Mrs Nightingale said. 'It's all good exercise.'

'Her tooth's as hard as rock,' Sophie said, wiping her brow and handing the file back to Violet.

'Harder,' said Tom. 'Can anything else open its mouth that wide?' he asked, staring at Harriet, whose mouth was still open.

'Hardly anything,' said Mrs Nightingale. 'A hippo can open its mouth 150 degrees. That's almost half a circle.'

Tom opened his mouth as wide as he could.

'Shall we file your teeth now, Tom?' Violet asked with a smile.

'Let's do it!' exclaimed Sophie. 'Pass me the file, Violet!'

Tom quickly closed his mouth again.

Chapter 3

That afternoon, after Dr Sharp and Violet had left, Tom and Sophie talked about nothing but teeth for at least half an hour. They went to the zoo shop and stood in the aisles for about fifteen minutes, flicking through the books to find any mentions of teeth.

'This one says that dolphins have more teeth than any other animal,' said Tom. 'They've got, like, two hundred!'

'It says in this book says that sharks lose and regrow their teeth every couple of weeks,' said Sophie, 'so they grow up to thirty thousand teeth in the course of a lifetime.'

'Thirty thousand teeth!' said Tom. 'Imagine how much money you'd get from the tooth fairy!'

Sophie snapped her book shut. 'We should help Dr Sharp.'

'What do you mean?' Tom asked.

'We should keep an eye on the zoo animals' teeth,' said Sophie. 'Monitor them every week. Check they're eating properly. Look out for any sore jaws.'

'OK,' said Tom, 'but how?'

'We'll take photos,' said Sophie. 'We'll talk to zookeepers. We'll analyse animal droppings. We'll video them eating their meals. We'll be Dental Detectives!'

'Tooth Sleuths,' added Tom.

'Youth Tooth Sleuths,' said Sophie.

They spent the rest of the afternoon going from one enclosure to the next, working out whether each animal had teeth and, if so, whether they needed to be monitored.

Sophie had a map of the zoo and placed a blue cross next to animals they knew didn't

have teeth and a red circle around those that belonged on their Patients' Register.

They paused in front of the giant Galapagos tortoises. One of the tortoises had a bunch of leaves sticking out of its mouth.

'They must have teeth, right?' Tom asked.

'No, I read about this earlier,' said Sophie. 'No tortoises have teeth.'

'But look, it's *chewing*,' said Tom.

'It breaks down its food with its strong beak and its tough jaws,' Sophie said. 'No teeth are involved.'

'So they're a bit like Grandad then?' Tom said with a grin.

Sophie grinned back and put a blue cross on the map next to the giant tortoises.

A few minutes later, they were staring at the Sumatran tigers.

'Now, they *definitely* have teeth,' said Tom.

'Yeah, I really hope they don't have any dental problems,' said Sophie. 'I wouldn't want to give one of them a filling.'

One of the tigers came towards them and

yawned, showing off its huge canines and razor-sharp back teeth. It was by far the smaller of the two tigers so Tom and Sophie knew it was Lizzie, the female.

'Wow, look at Liz,' said Tom. 'That book was right – *all* her teeth are sharp, even the ones at the back.'

'Look at how big her canines are,' Sophie said. 'They must be seven centimetres at least. I remember reading that a tiger's canines are really sensitive to pressure. That lets them work out exactly where to bite a deer's neck.'

Tom shuddered. 'Or a *person*'s neck,' he said.

'Tigers don't eat people,' said Sophie, rolling her eyes. 'I mean they *rarely* eat people.'

At that moment Tom spotted a pigeon strutting up and down beside the tigers' pool. 'Look, Soph,' he said, 'how did that get inside? It wasn't there a minute ago.'

'It must have squeezed in through the top of the enclosure somehow,' said Sophie, looking up.

'It's dead meat,' said Tom.

The male tiger had emerged from a cluster of shrubs, sniffing the air.

'Looks like Ziggy has woken up,' said Sophie.

'Yes, for his breakfast,' said Tom.

The pigeon was bending forward and pecking at the surface of the pool.

The male tiger crouched down, lowering its

body so its belly was nearly touching the ground. Then it took one step forward, moving slowly towards the bird.

'Wow, he moves just like Mindy and Max,' said Tom.

'I really don't want to see this,' said Sophie, putting her hands in front of her eyes but then peeking out.

Ziggy was staring fixedly at the pigeon. His feet made no sound as he moved across the stone floor of the enclosure.

The pigeon was strutting backwards and forwards again.

The tiger's steps were faster now, but still silent.

Tom and Sophie were on the verge of calling out. Shouldn't they warn the pigeon? Or should they not interfere?

At that instant, the tiger sprinted and pounced.

Miraculously, the pigeon flew up and away, finally perching in a distant corner of the enclosure.

Sophie was relieved. Tom was disappointed.

'I never get to see *anything* cool,' he huffed.

Mr Nightingale appeared behind them.

'What are you moaning about now, Tom?' he asked.

They explained what had just happened and pointed out the pigeon.

'Ah, I see,' said Mr Nightingale. 'I'd better try to get it out, I suppose.'

'Did you see him flash his teeth as he pounced?' Sophie said to Tom.

'Yeah,' said Tom, his eyes wide.

'Any . . . dental problems or issues?' she asked, looking down at her map and holding up her pen.

'Er, ah, I don't think so,' said Tom. 'I was kind of looking at the pigeon.'

'So you two are dentists now?' Mr Nightingale said with a smile. 'Well, don't you worry about Ziggy the Tiger. His teeth are one hundred and ten per cent healthy.'

Sophie put a red circle around the tigers' enclosure on her map and said, 'All done!'

Chapter 4

Over the next six Saturdays, Tom and Sophie took photos, kept journals and drew sketches. They assembled a huge number of pictures and descriptions of animals' teeth.

They hadn't thought much about teeth before; now they realised that, for most animals, teeth were a matter of life and death. They could be used for so many things – for chewing food, for defending yourself, for building your home, for carrying your young, for attracting a mate, for digging, for climbing, for lifting . . .

If your teeth weren't strong and healthy, then you wouldn't last long.

For the first couple of weeks, Tom and Sophie had nothing to report. The zoo animals were eating well and nobody's teeth were loose or wonky or a funny colour.

However, on the fourth Saturday, the Tooth Sleuths took on their first case. They were in Nightzone, visiting the bats. Bats were still among Tom and Sophie's favourite animals – ever since they had helped to rescue a baby bat a few months before.

This time now a different nocturnal animal caught their attention – Sammy the rat.

They were pressing their noses up against the rats' enclosure, watching them scampering along the branches and scuttling through the woodchips.

Tom was muttering to himself.

'What have you spotted, young assistant?' Sophie asked.

Tom replied, 'Hang on – I'm the dentist, *you're* the assistant.'

'No, that was last week,' Sophie said. 'This week *I'm* the dentist.'

Tom sighed and said, 'OK, *doctor*, I noticed that Sammy's chew toy is stuck under a rock. So he's got nothing to gnaw on and that could cause him tooth problems.'

'So that's why he didn't rush to get his food when the keepers put it out,' Sophie said. 'His teeth are probably overgrowing. Remember that rodents' teeth grow constantly.'

'Er, sort of,' said Tom.

'Rats' teeth grow their whole life,' Sophie continued. 'They never stop. In a year, their incisors – that's their front teeth – can grow up to twelve centimetres. That's longer than your fingers. Every year!'

'A sabre-toothed rat! Cool!' said Tom.

'No, no, that'd never happen,' said Sophie. 'For a start, they grind their teeth constantly. To file them down. That's why they get branches and wood blocks and chew toys. But that's not the main reason you never get a sabre-toothed rat.'

'What is then?' Tom asked.

'Well, it's a bit sad but . . .' Sophie said.

Tom looked worried. 'How sad?'

'A rat's teeth curl backwards if they grow too much,' Sophie said, 'so they only need to grow an extra half a centimetre before the rat finds it hard to eat. The rat will die long before its teeth start sticking out of its mouth.'

Sophie had drawn a sketch on her pad of a rat's teeth curling backwards.

'So you think that could happen to Sammy?' Tom said. 'He's lost his favourite chew toy so his teeth are starting to grow backwards and he can't eat?'

'I'm sure of it,' said Sophie, tapping her picture.

'We've got a serious crisis on our hands!' declared Tom.

'We have to remain calm,' said Sophie. 'Remember, Dr Sharp always remains calm. Even when he's got his arm in a hippo's mouth.'

'But Sammy could drop dead any minute!' exclaimed Tom. 'Imagine your teeth being a metre long and growing down your throat!'

'I read in a book that it's quite easy to trim a rat's teeth,' said Sophie. 'We just have to find a zookeeper.'

They spotted Terry the Nightzone keeper in the Malagasy jumping rat enclosure, scattering

food on the ground. They waved at him and beckoned him over.

'Hello, you two. What's up?' Terry asked, when he'd clambered out of the enclosure and emerged from a door marked 'ZOOKEEPERS ONLY'.

Sophie quickly explained that they were trainee dentists and that Sammy was in trouble.

Tom added that Sammy's teeth could grow down his throat and out of his back, sticking out like spears, and they might even stab other rats nearby, killing them too.

'Really? Sounds serious,' said Terry with a smile. 'Well, I did notice that Sammy was off his food yesterday. I was going to leave it one more day, then call on your mum. But I think you're right – it's his teeth. Let's take a closer look.'

Tom and Sophie followed Terry through the door reserved for zoo staff and were soon standing behind the rats' enclosure. Terry opened a small wooden panel and reached inside. After a bit of rummaging, he pulled out Sammy.

'Who wants to hold him?' Terry asked.

'Me!' Tom and Sophie both exclaimed.

'I should have known,' Terry said. 'OK, you can both have a go. To decide who goes first, answer me this. Roughly how many rats are there in the UK?'

'A million,' said Sophie.

'Ten million,' said Tom.

'Tom's closest,' said Terry. 'It's actually eighty million. There are more rats than human beings. So he goes first.'

Tom was so excited, he fumbled and nearly dropped Sammy.

'This is precisely why I should have gone first,' said Sophie.

But Tom calmed down and held Sammy firmly but gently. Terry opened the rat's mouth and looked closely at his teeth.

Sophie peered in too. Terry nodded and said, 'It's his bottom teeth, look.'

Sophie nodded. They were like tiny tusks, curling around till they almost touched his tongue.

'What are you going to do?' Tom asked.

In reply, Terry pulled something out of his pocket.

'What are they? Pliers or scissors or something?' Tom asked.

'Sort of,' said Terry, holding the tool up so both Tom and Sophie could see it. 'OK, it's Sophie's turn.'

So Sophie held Sammy while Terry snipped off the end of one of Sammy's lower incisors. Terry flicked the tooth-end on to his palm so Sammy didn't swallow it. Then he clipped off the end of the tooth next to it.

'Can I keep these?' Tom asked, picking up the two pieces of tooth.

'As long as Sammy doesn't want them,' Terry said with a smile.

Sammy was returned to the enclosure. Terry also pulled the chew toy out from under the rock and put it next to the feeding bowl.

'Thanks for your help,' said Terry, '*again.*'

Chapter 5

After a few weeks of being Youth Tooth Sleuths, Tom and Sophie felt that they had learned all there was to know about teeth.

'Maybe we should get into something else now,' Tom said. 'Eyes or fingers or something.'

'We haven't had any tooth mysteries to solve for at least two weeks,' said Sophie, nodding. 'I think maybe the animals' teeth will be fine without us.'

'We've been pestering the zookeepers about teeth too,' said Tom. 'Now they're looking out for tooth problems even more than we are.'

So, as Tom and Sophie walked across the picnic lawn at the zoo, they agreed that their work was probably done and that the animals didn't need their help any more in the dental department. They decided to celebrate with two hot chocolates plus squirty cream.

The tigers' enclosure was on the way to the cafe, so they stopped briefly to check out Ziggy.

He was lying on his side, yawning contentedly, about two metres away from where they were standing.

'Are tigers bigger than lions?' Tom asked.

Sophie nodded. 'They're the biggest cat. Siberian tigers can be over three metres long. That's bigger than a lion, a leopard, a jaguar, a cheetah, a puma, a serval, a caracal, an ocelot, a margay, a lynx and an oncilla.'

'Are they all types of cat or did you make some of them up?' Tom asked.

'They're all real cats,' said Sophie, 'though some of them might not exist for much longer.'

'What do you mean?'

'Well, a lot of cats live in forests and jungles,' said Sophie, 'and people keep chopping them down. There used to be thousands and thousands of Sumatran tigers. Now there are fewer than four hundred in the wild.'

'How do you remember all this stuff?' Tom said.

'It's written on that sign,' said Sophie, pointing, 'over there.'

Just at that moment, Tom heard a fluttering sound.

'I don't believe it,' he exclaimed, and tugged at Sophie's arm, pointing to the far end of the tigers' enclosure. Once again a pigeon had somehow managed to wriggle through the wire.

'We'd better call Dad,' said Sophie, pulling out her mobile phone.

'OK.' Tom nodded, and watched the pigeon as it landed just a few metres away from Ziggy. Tom glanced at Ziggy and then back at the pigeon. Surely, this time, Ziggy would catch it.

Sophie had got through to their Dad and told him about the pigeon. She hung up.

'Well, that's weird,' Tom said.

'What's weird?' Sophie asked.

'Look at Ziggy,' said Tom.

They both looked at what the tiger was doing. Or rather, what the tiger wasn't doing. He hadn't even noticed the pigeon. When he finally did, he looked at it and then looked away.

Mr Nightingale arrived.

'I don't believe it,' said Mr Nightingale. 'I've worked here for fifteen years, and only ever known two pigeons get into that enclosure. And you've been here to see them both!'

'Well, this one's not in any danger,' said Tom. 'I think Ziggy has become a vegetarian.'

'That's strange,' said Mr Nightingale, look-ing at the tiger and rubbing his chin.

51

Sophie glanced at the lump of meat that Ziggy was now batting backwards and forwards with his paws and then said, 'Dad, are Ziggy's teeth OK? He doesn't seem very interested in his breakfast.'

'I wasn't sure if it was just an upset stomach,' said Mr Nightingale, 'but there's been no vomiting or drowsiness. You could be right, Sophie – it might be his teeth.'

'Look at his jaw, Dad!' said Tom. 'There seems to be a small lump, just above his lip.'

Mr Nightingale nodded. 'Well spotted, Tom. We'd better give Dr Sharp a ring.'

Tom and Sophie looked at each other and smiled.

'Looks like we're still in business,' said Sophie.

Later that day, after the zoo had closed its gates, Tom, Sophie and Mr Nightingale were back at the tiger enclosure. This time, they had Dr Sharp and Violet in tow.

Mr Nightingale was about to explain what

the problem was, but Sophie had already started talking.

'So we've had no problems with Ziggy's teeth before now,' she said, holding up her notebook, 'but this morning we noticed that he was off his food and showed no interest in stalking a pigeon that had got into his enclosure.'

Dr Sharp looked at Sophie and smiled. 'So what do you think it could be?' he asked.

'Definitely a problem with the canines,' said Sophie.

'He has a slight swelling in his top lip,' said Tom, 'so if it's not the canines, it's the incisors.'

Dr Sharp peered into the enclosure and glanced back at Violet. Violet nodded.

'Ed, can we have a look at him in the hospital?' Dr Sharp asked.

Mr Nightingale nodded and said, 'I'll call Katie.'

While Mr Nightingale was phoning Mrs Nightingale, Ziggy seemed to notice that he was being watched. He stalked towards the edge of his enclosure where everybody was standing, not taking his eyes off Dr Sharp. He bared his front teeth in a snarl. This made Dr Sharp stare even harder, so Ziggy gave a full-on roar, showing all his teeth at once.

'What an extraordinary sight,' Dr Sharp said, 'Violet, did you see his canines?'

Violet nodded. 'I think Tom and Sophie are right. Either an incisor or a canine has become infected. His top gum looks tender and discoloured.'

Ziggy roared again, even louder. This time, he kept his teeth bared even after he had finished roaring.

Then he turned away sharply, swishing his tail back and forth.

'I'm pretty sure Ziggy doesn't want to go to the dentist,' said Tom. 'I recognise the signs.'

Dr Sharp nodded. 'I don't think he'll change his mind either. Fortunately your Mum's on her way.'

At that moment, Mrs Nightingale arrived.

'Are you sure you need Ziggy to be asleep?' she asked with a smile. 'He's just a big pussycat really.'

'We're sure,' Dr Sharp and Violet said together.

Mrs Nightingale called Ziggy and he looked up, seeming to recognise her voice. He walked slowly over to her and lay down alongside the mesh as if he was used to this routine. Mrs Nightingale took a syringe out of her case and quickly injected him in his rump. Ziggy didn't flinch. He just looked at Mrs Nightingale over his shoulder and then back at his enclosure.

'Doesn't that hurt him?' said Tom.

'Not at all,' said Mrs Nightingale. 'He barely felt it. Years ago, to put a tiger like Ziggy to sleep, I'd have had to use a tranquilliser gun. Seeing the rifle used to make all the cats panic. Ever seen a lion or a tiger panicking?'

'I don't think so,' said Sophie.

'You'd remember if you had,' said Mrs Nightingale. 'Anyway, we've trained them to let us do this instead.'

By this time, Ziggy was asleep.

'OK, let's get the patient to the hospital,' said Mr Nightingale.

Mrs Nightingale fastened an oxygen tube to Ziggy's mouth and attached monitor cables to his body so that she could keep an eye on his heartbeat and blood pressure. Then Mr Nightingale rolled the tiger on to a black hammock-like sheet and then, with help from Mrs Nightingale and another keeper, they lifted the tiger into the back of a zoo truck. Mr Nightingale squatted next to Ziggy and stroked him gently.

Tom and Sophie looked at their father expectantly.

'Oh, go on then,' Mr Nightingale said. 'In you get.'

So Tom and Sophie sat in the back of the van with their father as Ziggy was driven through the zoo to the hospital. 'He's so soft,' said Sophie, running her hands through his fur.

'When he's awake,' Mr Nightingale said, 'that fur is super-sensitive. It can detect the smallest pressure or faintest movement.'

'Look at his massive paws,' said Tom, stroking one of Ziggy's front legs.

'Those paws are pretty incredible too,' said Mr Nightingale. 'Like most other cats, he can decide when to show his claws and when to put them away. Imagine being able to move your fingernails in and out!'

Tom and Sophie looked down at Ziggy in wonder, their mouths open.

'There's – there's – no way he could wake up, is there?' Tom asked.

Mr Nightingale smiled and shook his head. 'It's not likely, and we'd get some warning. Chances are he'll wake up in about three hours, happy and rested.'

However, just at that moment, the truck went over a bump on the path and Ziggy seemed to stir.

Tom and Sophie sprang back against the side of the van.

'D-Dad . . .' stammered Tom, 'you said . . .'

A split second later, the van swerved to the left left and Ziggy appeared to lift up two of his legs.

'He moved, Dad. He moved!' Sophie exclaimed.

'For goodness' sake, you two,' Mr Nightingale said. 'It's just the movement of the van. He's fast asleep. Honestly.'

Mr Nightingale put his face next to Ziggy's. 'Sleeping like a baby!' he said.

Sophie smiled and relaxed.

Tom calmed down slightly, but stayed right against the side of the van, one arm on the door handle.

A couple of minutes later they reached the hospital. Mr Nightingale and some vets carried Ziggy carefully in through the door and along the corridor before gently laying him on an operating table.

Mrs Nightingale checked his oxygen supply and the monitor cables.

Tom and Sophie were allowed to stand in the room next door and watch through a glass screen. There was a speaker above them, so they could also hear everything that Dr Sharp, Mrs Nightingale and Violet were saying.

Everyone in the operating room put on a mask and gown, scrubbed their hands and pulled on gloves. Then they turned back to Ziggy.

'OK, let's start with a general check-up,' Dr Sharp said.

He gently tugged on Ziggy's huge tongue – which stretched as if it was made of rubber. At the same time, Mrs Nightingale carefully held

Ziggy's mouth wide open, so Dr Sharp could see right into the back of the tiger's mouth.

Dr Sharp tapped and scraped with a long metal tool.

'A tiger's back teeth are called carnassials. They're very strong and very sharp. They're not round and flat like our molars because tigers don't really *chew* as such. They just tear meat off and swallow.'

Dr Sharp nodded at Violet. 'All fine there. Let's take a closer look at that upper canine.'

He lifted Ziggy's upper lip.

'Now, a tiger's canines are the longest of any cat,' Dr Sharp continued. 'Longer than a lion's, longer than a jaguar's. They're about fifteen centimetres, and their roots go right up into the tiger's skull.'

Violet whispered something to Dr Sharp and he nodded.

'That's true, the clouded leopard's tigers are longer in relation to its body size,' he said. 'Good point, Violet.'

He peered underneath Ziggy's lip and inspected his gums.

'The thing is though,' said Dr Sharp, 'tigers' teeth aren't so different to ours. They get plaque like we do. They can need fillings too. And, as in this case, they can also get infections.'

Tom looked at Sophie with a worried expression. An infection sounded bad.

'The infection has spread into his gum and, if we don't intervene, it could spread through his whole body and make him very sick indeed,' Dr Sharp said.

Sophie looked back at Tom, also worried.

'So at least we know he's got an infected canine. What's the plan?' Mrs Nightingale asked.

'A pretty basic procedure,' replied Violet. 'It's called root canal work.'

'Oh, OK,' Mrs Nightingale said, nodding. 'You did that to me last year.'

'What that means,' said Violet, glancing up at Tom and Sophie through the glass, 'is that we'll remove the pulp in the centre of Ziggy's canine. All mammals – humans included – have pulp tissue down the inside of each of their teeth. It supplies the tooth with nutrients and helps with feeling and sensation. But sometimes this pulp gets infected. Bacteria spreads through the tooth, killing the pulp tissue. So we have to clean the pulp out and replace it. That way, the tooth can survive for another ten years or more.'

Dr Sharp was holding a metal tool with a long needle on the end.

'Ready, Violet?' he asked.

Violet nodded.

Dr Sharp started by hollowing out the end of Ziggy's canine with the needle. Then he took a long thin tube and threaded it up the centre of the tooth. He kept passing it further and further up.

'When's he going to get to the end?' Tom asked.

Sophie shrugged. 'He said it was a really long tooth.'

Finally Dr Sharp stopped pushing and wiggled the tube around to remove all of the infected pulp.

A few minutes later, Dr Sharp stood aside and Violet moved in, filling the centre of the tooth with a greyish material. Throughout, Ziggy looked peaceful and oblivious, his gigantic tongue lolling out of the side of his mouth and resting on the operating table.

'OK, let's put the crown on,' said Dr Sharp.

'A crown?' Tom whispered to Sophie, pointing at his head

'Not that kind of crown, you dingbat,' Sophie said. 'A crown for his tooth.'

Tom looked confused.

'A crown is an artificial tooth,' Violet said. 'We're going to stick it on to replace the top of Ziggy's tooth. It will look just like a real one.'

The children watched as the dentist filed down Ziggy's tooth to make room for the crown. Then Violet squirted dental cement on to the end of Ziggy's canine. She passed

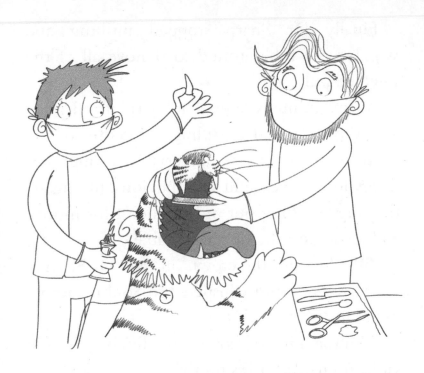

Dr Sharp the crown and he carefully pressed it
into place. The crown was made of white plastic and was a very good match. Tom and Sophie
couldn't tell where the tooth ended and the
crown began.

'All done,' Dr Sharp said.

'You can take him back home now,' added
Violet.

Tom and Sophie met Dr Sharp and Violet in the corridor outside the operating theatre.

'Will Ziggy's mouth be sore?' Sophie asked.

'For a little bit,' Dr Sharp said, 'but he'll be back on the steak by tomorrow.'

'Do you want to come and celebrate with us?' Tom asked. 'Before we spotted that Ziggy was sick, we were actually on our way to have hot chocolate and squirty cream.'

'Hot chocolate is full of sugar,' Dr Sharp exclaimed, 'and sugar rots your teeth!'

'Oh, yeah, I suppose . . .' Tom admitted.

'However,' said the dentist went on, 'it's not every day you have a tiger for a patient. So let's all have hot chocolate *and* some cake too!'

'Hot chocolate and cake!' exclaimed Violet.

Tom and Sophie grinned.

Chapter 6

Over the next few days, Tom and Sophie kept a close eye on Ziggy. They visited him every day after school. Tom took lots of photographs and Sophie drew sketches and made notes.

'He's completely back to normal, isn't he?' Tom said on the third afternoon, as they watched Ziggy gnawing on a gigantic bone.

'He seems to be,' said Sophie.

'It's funny what Dr Sharp said about tigers not chewing their food,' said Tom. 'I read on the internet that tigers can't even move their jaws from side to side. Just up and down. They bite and then they swallow.'

They watched Ziggy nibbling and tearing tiny bits of meat off the tip of the bone with his front teeth.

'Ah, hello, you two,' said a voice behind them.

They turned around and saw their grandad leaning on his walking stick.

'I thought I'd find you here,' he said.

'Everything OK, Grandad?' Sophie asked.

'Funny you should ask,' he replied, 'because I think I might need your help.'

Both Tom and Sophie turned to face him.

'I've heard a rumour that you know rather a lot about teeth,' said Grandad.

Sophie blushed and said, 'Sort of.'

Tom said, 'We know absolutely everything! We saved that tiger's life!'

'Glad to hear it,' said Grandad. 'The thing is, we've been having a few problems over at the allotment. Probably better if I just show you, eh? That is, if you're not busy here.'

'No, we've fixed most of the zoo animals,'

Tom said, 'We're so good, we've run out of patients.'

'Tom, that's not completely true,' said Sophie.

'I bet it is true!' Grandad exclaimed. 'Knowing you two! Come on, let me show you the crime scene.'

Grandad, Tom and Sophie went around behind the zoo cafe, through the staff turnstile and out into Regent's Park. Grandad had previously been Chief Vet at London Zoo and he was still allowed to use the staff exits and short cuts.

'Now, as you probably know,' Grandad said as they walked, 'I work in the Regents' Park allotments a couple of evenings a week. We grow all kinds of things: flowers, herbs, vegetables, fruit bushes. It's a gardener's paradise in there. But last night we had a break-in.'

Grandad led Tom and Sophie towards the allotment and opened a small brown gate. He showed them a row of half-eaten cabbages and what had been a row of broccoli. Everywhere there were small holes, disturbed soil and mangled plants.

Then he led them into the shed at the end of the allotment and showed them the remains of a ham sandwich on the floor.

'I was saving that sandwich for my supper,' Grandad said, 'but when I woke up, this was all that was left of it.'

'You mean, you were in here?' Tom asked.

'Ah, er, yes,' Grandad stammered, 'just having a nap. I'd been hard at work, you see! So anyway, it happened at about eight o'clock at night. Whatever it was must be a nocturnal animal. Let me show you how he got in.'

They went back outside and he took Tom and Sophie round behind the shed.

The panel at the back had a small hole at the bottom, with claw marks at the edges. A section of the fence had also been nibbled away by very strong teeth.

'Look at these bite marks here,' said Grandad, pulling up the loose board at the bottom of the

fence and showing Tom and Sophie the other
side. A ring of teeth marks could clearly be seen
in the wood.

'The thing is,' Grandad said, 'I can't think of
a single British animal that would leave teeth
marks like that. Particularly not one that eats
flowers *and* vegetables *and* ham sandwiches.'

'Right then, Soph,' said Tom. 'We've got a
new case.'

Sophie nodded. 'Time to take a look at the
evidence.'

Tom and Sophie were standing on the outside of the allotment fence. Sophie was running her finger along the teeth marks in the wood.

'Could it have been a cat?' Tom asked.

'Not sure,' said Sophie.

'All cats have similar teeth, right?' Tom said. 'These teeth marks are like a smaller version of a tiger's – a bit like our pet cats', in fact. Two big holes for the canines, two smaller holes for the incisors.'

Tom felt the bottom of the fence.

'A cat's back teeth could have gnawed along the bottom here,' he added.

Sophie didn't agree. 'These marks are too shallow and close together,' she said. 'A cat's teeth are giant compared to whatever did this.'

'If you say so,' said Tom.

'I do say so,' said Sophie.

'So how are we going to find out what broke into the allotment?' Tom asked.

Sophie was silent for a few seconds.

'If only we could make some kind of model of those teeth marks,' Sophie said.

'You mean like a set of fake teeth?' Tom said. 'Like those vampire fangs you can buy at Halloween.'

'Exactly,' Sophie said. 'Then we could ask the keepers at the zoo if they recognise the teeth in the model. If they do, we'll know which animal broke in.'

They were both silent for another few seconds, thinking.

'Violet . . .' whispered Tom.

'What do you mean, Violet?' Sophie asked.

'Last time I went to the dentist,' Tom said, 'Dr Sharp had this model of a human being's teeth. Made out of shiny white plastic or something. While he was telling me about my teeth, he was pointing to the teeth in the model.'

'Yeah, he did that with me too. So?' Sophie said.

'He said that Violet had made the whole thing,' said Tom, 'and that she'd modelled it on her own teeth!'

'Wow! Really?' Sophie said.

'I bet she could show us how to do it,' Tom said.

Sophie pulled out her mobile phone and rang the dentist's surgery. She apologised for disturbing Dr Sharp and Violet, but said this was an emergency.

Ten minutes later, Violet was crouching down next to Tom and Sophie, studying the teeth marks in the fence closely. She had her blue dentist's case with her.

'Luckily I finish early on Fridays,' said Violet, 'so we can take our time.'

She looked at the fence again.

'So we're going to make a dental cast, are we?' Violet said. 'Brilliant. First of all we need to find a nice clean set of bite marks. Both the upper and lower teeth. Here we are.'

She pointed to the underside of the fence.

'Usually what I'd do is get the patient to bite down on a lump of wax-like material and then make the cast out of the impression they leave behind. But in this case I'll make the cast directly from the marks in the wood.'

She poured some white powder into the teeth marks on one side of the fence. Tom and Sophie watched as she added water and other chemicals and, within a few minutes, there was a lump of wet clay-like material sitting on the wood.

'While that's drying, I'll do the bottom set.'

She repeated the process.

'Easy, eh?' Violet said.

The cast for the top set of teeth was almost dry. She held it up.

'Wow,' said Tom, 'look how sharp those canines are.'

'I have to admit,' said Violet, 'I'm not entirely sure who these belong to.'

'I thought they looked like a cat's teeth, but now I think they look like Felicity's,' said Tom.

Violet looked blank, so he added, 'Felicity is our ferret.'

'Interesting,' said Violet, 'so we're thinking – a relation of the ferret. What time is it?'

Sophie glanced down at her phone. 'Four thirty.'

'Great,' said Violet, 'the zoo's still open for another hour. Let's nip inside and do some more research.'

'Cool!' exclaimed Tom and Sophie.

As they trotted away from the allotment, Grandad called out, 'Have you solved the case yet?'

'Almost!' Tom called back, 'Just heading for the zoo. We've got a new lead!'

When they reached the zoo, Violet asked Tom and Sophie to think about any animals that might have the same body type or the same diet as a ferret.

'The meerkats!' exclaimed Tom.

'The mongooses!' suggested Sophie.

'The otters!' declared Tom.

So they looked at the meerkats and the mongooses in Animal Adventure and the otters next to the Rainforest Lookout. Finally they examined all the rodents in the Nightzone. None of them matched.

'All the animals have similar teeth,' said Violet, holding up the dental cast, 'but none of them are exactly the same.'

'Well, they've got to belong to *something*,' said Tom, looking puzzled.

As they went to leave, Terry the Nightzone Keeper was coming in.

'Hello, you two,' he said. 'Come to see how the rats are doing?'

'Hi, Terry,' said Tom and Sophie. 'This is Violet.'

Sophie explained what they were doing.

'Let's have a look,' he said, taking the dental cast and peering closely at it.

'It's not a cat or a ferret or a mongoose,' Tom said.

Terry shook his head, 'No, it isn't.'

'We thought it looked like a mini-tiger,' said Sophie, 'with canines like that.'

'You're not far off,' said Terry.

'You mean, you know what it is?' Violet said.

'I think so,' said Terry. 'I reckon it's a polecat.'

'So it *is* a cat,' Tom said.

'No, a polecat's not a cat,' said Terry. 'In fact, it's closely related to your pet ferret. There used to be hardly any left in the wild, but there are more and more these days. I didn't realise they'd got as far south as London, but it seems they have.'

'But why would a polecat be on Grandad's allotment?' asked Tom. 'They don't eat vegetables, do they?'

'Definitely not. Look at these teeth again,' said Terry. 'A polecat is a pure predator. Its skull is only about four centimetres deep, so these teeth are huge compared to the size of its head. And feel, these canines are like knives.'

Tom ran his finger over the cast and felt the two top canine teeth.

'Like a tiger, a polecat uses its canines to deliver the killer blow at the base of its victim's neck,' said Terry. 'And like a tiger, the sharpness of these teeth means that it can take on prey that is much bigger than itself. Rabbits, chickens, even geese. One bite and it's over. And it can use its teeth more cleverly too.'

'What do you mean?' Sophie asked.

'If there's lots of prey about,' said Terry, 'and it can't possibly eat them all, it just paralyses them.'

'How?' Tom asked.

'It bites into its victim's brain, but not enough to kill it. Then it drags the body back to its den to eat later. But because it's still technically alive, it stays fresh.'

'That is brilliant,' said Tom, impressed.

'So it attacks everything and anything,' said Sophie, 'even when it's not particularly hungry.'

Terry nodded and glanced at the dental cast again.

'And this one is young and healthy,' said Terry. 'No nicked or broken teeth, very little decay.'

'Then it's obvious what happened,' said Sophie.

'Is it?' Violet and Tom said at the same time.

'Well, there's no way the polecat would have wanted to eat the vegetables in the allotment,' said Sophie, 'not with teeth like that.'

'What then?' asked Tom.

'There must have been another animal in the allotment,' said Sophie. 'Another animal was eating the vegetables. And the polecat wanted to eat that other animal.'

Tom nodded and said, 'Yes . . .'

'Wow, aren't you clever!' Violet added.

'But how did that *other* animal get in?' Tom asked.

'THAT's what we've got to find out,' said Sophie. 'Come on, back to the allotment.'

She sped off, calling out, 'Thanks, Terry,' over her shoulder.

'Yeah, thanks, Terry,' Tom called too, following his sister.

'Let me know when you solve the case!' Terry exclaimed.

'We will!' the children replied, their voices echoing in the cold evening air.

Chapter 7

Tom and Sophie and Violet were back at the allotment, staring at the hole in the fence. Tom was rubbing his chin. Sophie had her hands on her hips. Violet was scratching her head.

'So if another animal was here before the polecat,' Tom said, 'how did it get in? There are no other gaps in the fence.'

'It has to be something that's good at climbing. Or jumping,' said Violet.

A moment later, a pigeon landed on the top of the fence.

Sophie and Violet smiled and looked at each other.

'Or flying,' they said together.

Tom looked up too.

'Of course,' he said, 'the allotment must be full of seeds – Grandad's always planting new stuff. A pigeon would love that. And look.'

He pointed at a trail of white streaks that had run down the fence and dried out.

'Bird poo,' he said. 'It looks as if they perch up there all the time. They must wait till the allotment is quiet or empty and then fly in and eat the seeds.'

'So the polecat smells the pigeon,' said Sophie.

'It thinks – I'm going to bite his brain and save him for the weekend,' said Tom.

'If the pigeon was strutting back and forth on the other side of the fence,' said Violet, 'then the smell and the sound would have driven the polecat crazy. That would explain the depth and ferocity of the teeth marks.'

Just then, Grandad Nightingale appeared.

'Back from the zoo, then?' he said. 'What did you find out?'

'It's a polecat,' said Tom.

'A polecat!' said Grandad, raising his eyebrows. 'Well, I never. I'd never have guessed that. You never used to get them in this part of the country. And aren't they carnivores?'

'Yes, but we think he was chasing a pigeon!' Tom announced.

'But what about the bite marks in the cabbage,' Grandad said, 'and the dug-up flowers. Why would a polecat do that? As soon as it got through the fence, the pigeon would have flown off, wouldn't it?'

'Hmm,' said Violet, 'we'd better look at the other bite marks. The ones in the cabbages.'

Grandad led them to the far side of the allotment. Although the evening was drawing in, Tom, Sophie and Violet could still just about make out the dents and hollows that had been left in the vegetables. Sophie ran her finger along the edge of a half-eaten cabbage.

'It's definitely been gnawed,' she said, 'not bitten into.'

'So whatever did this,' Tom said, 'was more like a rat. Remember how they only have chewing teeth.'

Violet nodded. 'There are no canine teeth marks here. This animal doesn't have teeth for tearing flesh.'

'A herbivore then,' Sophie said, getting up. 'So not a polecat. A completely different animal.'

'But which animal?' Tom said, getting frustrated. 'We know there was a pigeon in here.

But a bird didn't do this. They don't even have teeth.' Then he realised that he wasn't completely sure this was true. 'Do they?' he asked Violet.

'No, they don't,' said Violet with a smile. 'They just peck, gulp, swallow.'

'So there was a *third* animal,' said Sophie, holding her chin and peering into the distance.

'Let's look for more clues!' exclaimed Tom.

He started to rummage around among the chewed–up lettuces and half-eaten radishes.

Violet and Sophie also got down on their hands and knees.

'Look for footprints, droppings, anything,' Sophie said, as she began to look around.

After a few minutes Tom stood up and held out a long stick. 'Look at this,' he said. 'More gnawing.'

Violet and Sophie got up and looked. It was a small branch from a nearby tree, and they could see that much of the bark had been chewed off. The wood underneath had scrape and scoop marks in it.

'This is great stuff, Tom,' said Violet. 'This means we know we're looking for an animal that needs to gnaw branches to stop its teeth growing too long.'

'Look at the teeth marks, Violet,' said Sophie. 'Two long parallel grooves. So this animal had two large front teeth.'

'A rabbit!' both children said together.

Violet nodded. 'Almost certainly.'

'But if there was a rabbit in here, why didn't the polecat eat it?' Tom asked, looking confused.

'Hmm,' said Sophie. 'Let's go to Grandad's shed and look at all of our evidence. We know that a polecat, a pigeon and a rabbit visited the allotment last night. We've just got to piece together how it all happened.'

Tom, Sophie, Violet and Grandad were in the shed looking at three pebbles on an old wooden table.

'OK, Grandad, are you paying attention?' Sophie asked.

'Absolutely,' Grandad replied, putting on a large pair of glasses that made his eyes look gigantic.

'So this brown pebble is the pigeon,' Sophie explained, 'this black pebble is the polecat, and this speckled one is the rabbit.'

'And this is the fence,' said Tom, stretching a piece of string across the table.

'I must say, this is all very imaginative,' said Grandad. 'It's almost as if I'm there.'

'You are, Grandad,' said Sophie. 'This is meant to be the allotment.'

'Oh yes, oh yes,' said Grandad, 'of course. Go on.'

'OK, so a pigeon lands on the fence . . .' Sophie started.

Tom moved the pigeon pebble on to the string.

'Polecat spots the pigeon, sprints towards the fence, pigeon flies into the allotment,' Sophie continued.

Tom moved the pigeon pebble into the allotment and placed the polecat pebble on the string.

'Polecat starts to tunnel under the fence, biting the wood in several places.'

Violet placed her dental cast on the table. 'We made this from the teeth marks,' she explained.

Grandad picked up at the cast and stared at it in amazement.

'When the polecat got through the fence, the pigeon spotted it and flew away,' said Sophie.

Tom took the pigeon pebble off the table and put it in his pocket.

'There was nothing else in the allotment that the polecat could eat,' said Sophie, 'but he could smell Grandad's sandwiches. So he came into the shed and ate them.'

Tom put one of Grandad's half-eaten sandwiches on the table and showed how the teeth from the cast fitted into the bite marks.

'After finishing his meal, the polecat goes home,' said Sophie, 'but a rabbit has found the hole that the polecat has made and, smelling the vegetables, he wriggles through.'

Tom put the polecat pebble into his pocket and moved the rabbit pebble over the string into the allotment.

'The rabbit tucked into some lettuces and cabbages,' said Sophie, 'and also sharpened his teeth on this stick.'

Tom laid the gnawed stick on the table.

'At that moment, Grandad wakes up,' said Sophie.

Tom placed an earthworm on the table.

Sophie giggled. 'Is that meant to be Grandad?'

'Ran out of stones,' said Tom with a shrug.

'The moment Grandad gets up out of his chair,' Sophie continued, 'the rabbit hears the noise and runs away. So when Grandad comes out into the allotment, all he sees are dug-up vegetables and the hole in the fence.'

'Goodness me, that's very clever,' said Grandad, 'and you worked out all of that just from looking at all the different teeth marks.'

Tom and Sophie nodded.

'I'm going to be out of a job at this rate,' said Violet.

At that moment, Sophie heard a noise and turned her head. She held a finger to her lips and pointed outside to the allotment.

'Out there,' she whispered.

It was now evening and the allotment was no more than a few grey outlines and dark shapes. Tom and Sophie moved quietly outside. Violet and Grandad followed them.

'We have to be as quiet as tigers on the prowl,' said Tom.

They headed silently towards the noise. When they were a few metres away, they stopped.

'Look,' whispered Sophie. 'He's brought some of his friends this time.'

There were three rabbits happily gnawing at Grandad's vegetables, their white tails bobbing and twitching.

Grandad watched for a few seconds and then

stepped forward abruptly. 'OK, you've filled your stomachs. Now be off with you!'

The rabbits scampered away.

'Better mend the hole in that fence,' he said.

Tom and Sophie smiled at each other and then at Grandad.

'Case closed,' said Tom.

Chapter 8

The following weekend, Tom and Sophie were sitting in Dr Sharp's waiting room. Tom had already been in for a check-up; Sophie was waiting for her name to be called.

'I can't believe I didn't need a filling,' Tom said. 'It's so unfair.'

'What do you mean?' Sophie replied. 'Surely that's good?'

'I wanted a filling,' Tom said, 'or even better, root canal treatment. Just like Ziggy.'

'But that'd really hurt!' insisted Sophie.

'It wouldn't hurt me,' Tom said. 'I'm going to come back to Dr Sharp's next week. And the week after. Until he finds something that he can drill or pull out or fill in.'

Sophie sighed. 'Look, I know it's been fun learning about teeth. But maybe we should find you another hobby.'

'No way,' said Tom. 'It's teeth all the way for me. So I can operate on tigers like Dr Sharp does. Or make casts and solve crimes like Violet.'

Sophie looked out the window and sighed. Mrs Nightingale had been chatting to the receptionist and was now walking back towards Tom and Sophie.

'Hey, guess what?' Mrs Nightingale said. 'Laura the receptionist is going on holiday next week.'

Tom looked up blankly. 'Lucky her.'

'She keeps parrots,' Mrs Nightingale continued. 'She's got an African grey parrot, a double yellow-headed Amazon and a green-winged macaw. She's found someone for the first two while she's on holiday, but she can't find anyone to look after the macaw.'

Tom stared at his mother in disbelief. 'Really?'

'Really,' said Mrs Nightingale. 'If you like the idea, then it will be coming to live on our boat for a couple of weeks.'

Tom started to hop from one leg to another. 'This is brilliant, this is brilliant,' he chanted.

Sophie was smiling too. She looked at Tom and said, 'Are you sure you want to look after a parrot?'

'Yeah, course,' said Tom. 'Why wouldn't I?'

'Well, they haven't got any teeth, have they?' Sophie said.

Tom stopped hopping for a couple of seconds. Then he started again.

'Yeah, but they can *talk*,' said Tom. 'There's only one thing better than an animal with teeth and that's an animal that can talk.'

He was skipping around the room now.

'I'm going to teach it to say, "Tom is brilliant" and "Tom's the best" and "There's Smelly Sophie."'

Sophie and Mrs Nightingale watched Tom

as he kept hopping around and muttering about all the things that we was going to teach the macaw to say.

'Maybe this wasn't such a good idea,' Mrs Nightingale said to Sophie.

'At least he's not going on about teeth any more,' Sophie said.

Mrs Nightingale and Sophie grinned at each other. Tom looked across and grinned too.

'It's funny,' said Mrs Nightingale, 'animals use their teeth to bite, chew, carry, dig and a hundred different other things. But that's not the best thing you can do with them. Not in my opinion.'

'So what is the best thing you can do with your teeth?' Tom asked, stopping for a moment.

'Smile,' said Mrs Nightingale, as her grin turned into a burst of laughter.

TIGER
TERRITORY

Open Now!

Have you been inspired by this exciting story?
See real-life tigers at ZSL London Zoo!
Visitors to the new **Tiger Territory** will see
a pair of endangered Sumatran tigers, Jae Jae
and Melati, in their fantastic Indonesian-inspired
home, which has been designed to make sure
it's perfect for the big cats.

ZSL London Zoo is home to world-leading
tiger experts, and has been home to tigers
for more than 100 years. Come down
to brand new **Tiger Territory**,
see our two new tiger friends and learn
more about these fascinating animals.

Tigers Gorillas

zsl.org/tigerterritory

Zoological Society of London

ZSL London Zoo is a very famous part of the
Zoological Society of London (ZSL).

For almost two hundred years, we have been
working tirelessly to provide hope and a
home to thousands of animals.

And it's not just the animals at ZSL's Zoos in
London and Whipsnade that we are caring for.
Our conservationists are working in more than
50 countries to help protect animals in the wild.

But all of this wouldn't be possible without your help.
As a charity we rely entirely on the generosity of our
supporters to continue this vital work.

By buying this book, you have made an essential
contribution to help protect animals.
Thank you.

Find out more at **zsl.org**

ZSL
**LONDON
ZOO**

ZSL
**WHIPSNADE
ZOO**

A bat is in peril! Join Tom and Sophie
as they brave the night's terrors.
Can they keep their favourite
nocturnal resident safe?

Turn the page for a taster from another
exciting adventure with the animal crackers
Nightingale family!

Chapter 1

Tom and Sophie Nightingale were on their way back from the cinema with their grandad. They had all been to see *AstroKid v The Man-Eating Martians* in 3D and were talking about the amazing special effects. They had just stepped on to the towpath that led down to the marina where they all lived, when every light in the area went out.

The lamp posts along the canal flickered and died, the houseboats in the marina were thrown into darkness and the houses along the edge of Regent's Park were suddenly swallowed up by the night.

'It's the man-eating Martians!' exclaimed Tom. 'They must be here!'

'Don't be daft, Tom,' replied his big sister, Sophie. 'It's just a power cut.'

'So what do we do now?' Tom wailed. 'How are we going to fight the Martians when we can't even see them?'

'It'll be OK, Tom,' Grandad replied, clapping Tom on the back and making him jump. 'We just have to use our other senses, that's all.'

'What do you mean, "our other senses"?' Tom asked.

'Our sense of hearing, our sense of touch,' said Grandad. 'Millions of creatures wake up at night. Bats, owls, hedgehogs, badgers . . . and they get around just fine.'

'How's hearing going to help?' Tom asked. 'I can't hear anything.'

'Course you can,' said Grandad. 'Just listen.' He tapped on the path with his walking stick. 'Hear that?'

'It sounds like concrete,' said Tom.

'Exactly. So we know we're on the path. You try.'

He reached for Tom's arm in the darkness and placed his walking stick in his grandson's hand.

Tom began to tap the path and move slowly forward.

After a few seconds, he exclaimed, 'I can do it!'

At the same time, Sophie said, 'My eyes are beginning to adjust. I think I can see our barge.' She reached out with one arm. 'Yes, I can feel the railings by our section of the towpath.'

'That's the idea,' Grandad said. He took a deep breath. 'And I can smell the ivy that grows along the bank.'

They all moved towards the side of the marina where the houseboats were moored.

Tom and Sophie lived with their parents on

a barge called the *Jessica Rose* but generally known as *The Ark*. If it hadn't been for the power cut, it would have been possible to see all the animals painted on the sides of the boat. The surrounding water had been worked into the design too, so there were hippos wallowing in it, penguins diving into it, elephants drinking from it and flamingos wading in it.

A few metres further along from *The Ark*, the next dark shape was Grandad's houseboat, the *Molly Magee*.

Tom gave Grandad his walking stick back and said, 'I think I can do this last bit.' Then he felt for the edge of *The Ark* with his foot and launched himself into the air.

'Tom!' Sophie exclaimed.

'What?' replied the voice of Tom in the darkness. 'It's fine. I'm totally used to the dark now. Come on – the door's down here.'

At that moment, the edge of the houseboat door glowed and opened. Mrs Nightingale was standing there, holding a candle.

'Hello, you three,' she said.

Tom and Sophie walked carefully down the steps.

'I'm going to check on my place,' said Grandad. 'See you in a bit.'

'Bye, Grandad,' said Tom.

'Thanks for taking us to the cinema,' added Sophie.

As Tom and Sophie entered the living room, Rex, the family terrier, ran up to greet them, sniffing and snuffling at Tom's shoes and trousers.

Sophie gave Rex a quick pat and then hurried to check on her ferret and her rats. She returned after a few seconds with a rat on her shoulder. 'They're all fine, especially Eric. I think rats must quite like the dark.'

In the meantime, Mrs Nightingale was

rummaging in the cupboard under the sink, looking for more candles.

'Where's Dad?' Tom asked.

'Your father is out on the bank, trying to get our emergency generator to work.' She emerged from the cupboard with a pair of candles and a box of matches. 'Last time he went near it, it caught fire twice and burnt off one of his eyebrows.'

'Oh, OK,' said Tom. 'What are those?'

He was pointing at a helmet with a pair of binoculars strapped to it.

'They're night vision goggles,' Mrs Nightingale said. 'I found them at the back of our wardrobe. I thought they might help your father fix the generator but naturally he left them behind.'

'Brilliant!' exclaimed Tom. He grabbed the helmet and slid it on to his head, fiddling with the chinstrap.

'You'd better not break them before I've had a go,' Sophie said.

Tom was squinting through the binoculars.

'You can see everything!' he exclaimed. 'And it turns everyone into a Martian. Rex and Eric have gone bright green. But, you know, that's kind of cool as well.'

He swung around, narrowly avoiding whacking Sophie with the binoculars.

'Mum, Grandad was talking about animals that wake up at night,' Tom said. 'Is this how they see?'

'In some cases,' said Mrs Nightingale. 'What happens is, those goggles magnify all the available light. There's infrared light coming from the other side of the canal out there, but it's too dim for us to see just with our eyes. But when you put those goggles on, they take all those tiny points of light and make them much, much brighter.'

'So that's what nocturnal animals do?' Tom asked.

'Some of them,' said Mrs Nightingale. 'Take owls, for instance. Their eyes are huge – they take up most of their skull. In fact, their eyes are so big that they can't even move them. That's why they have to twist their heads around.'

'Wow,' said Tom.

'In those huge eyes,' Mrs Nightingale went on, 'they have these amazing cells that can pick up the tiniest dots of light. We have them too, but they have ten times as many – which means they can see a hundred times better than us at night.'

'Wow,' said Tom again. 'And is everything green for them as well?'

'No, that's just those goggles,' said his mum with a smile.

'It must be my turn now,' complained Sophie.

Mrs Nightingale nodded. 'Give them to your sister, Tom.'

Tom groaned and took the helmet off.

Sophie handed Eric to her mother and fastened

the helmet chinstrap. Mrs Nightingale returned the rat to his cage and then came back to the living room.

Tom had been thinking.

'I wish I was a nocturnal animal,' he said.

'Hang on,' Mrs Nightingale said. 'Not all nocturnal animals have adapted like owls. Think about bats or moles. Their vision has got worse, not better. Mind you, their other senses have developed to compensate.'

'Oh yeah, Grandad said that,' Tom said.

'Moles are my favourite,' Mrs Nightingale said. 'They have an amazing sense of touch. They can sense the tiniest vibration in the soil around them.'

'Cool,' said Tom. 'Being a human is rubbish at night-time, that's for sure.'

'Mum, look, over there!' Sophie said, pointing at the window and squinting through the goggles at the other side of the canal.

'We can't see anything, can we?' Tom said, rolling his eyes.

Sophie pulled off the helmet and handed it to her mother.

'Something's fallen in the canal and it can't get out,' Sophie said. 'It looks like a puppy.'

Mrs Nightingale looked through the binoculars. She saw a small mammal, scrabbling at the sides of the canal, desperate to find a foothold in the brickwork.

'It's a young fox,' said Mrs Nightingale. 'It must have misjudged a jump. Foxes are good swimmers, but it looks like this one's struggling.'

'We've got to help it,' said Sophie.

'Sometimes it's best not to interfere with nature, Sophie,' said Mrs Nightingale.

'But that's your job, isn't it?' Sophie protested. 'Vets interfere with nature all the time.'

'Hmm,' said Mrs Nightingale. 'You do have a point.'

'Cool, let's go,' said Tom. 'It's got to be better than staying here in the pitch black waiting for the telly to work. Besides, we practised moving around in the dark with Grandad and I was brilliant at it.'

Sophie had already put her coat on and was standing by the door. Mrs Nightingale blew out the candles on the table. She took a pair of torches out of a kitchen drawer and put one in her pocket. She gave the other to Sophie.

Tom had picked up the night vision goggles and was strapping them on.

'What are you doing, Tom?' Mrs Nightingale asked.

'They'll help us to see the fox,' said Tom.

Mrs Nightingale thought for a moment. 'Well, those goggles belong to the zoo, so you have to be very careful.'

'Course,' said Tom, and walked out of the door, banging the top of the helmet on the frame and knocking a pot plant off a window ledge with the binoculars.

Mrs Nightingale picked up the pieces with a sigh and ordered Rex into his basket.

Then the three of them stepped on to the towpath.

ZSL
LONDON
ZOO

ZOO STORY

CATCH that BAT!

Adam Frost

Illustrated by
Mark Chambers

BLOOMSBURY

OUT NOW

More amazing behind-the-scenes animal action
at London Zoo
with the Nightingale family!

Stop! There's a Snake in Your Suitcase!
by Adam Frost

What's that slithering by the canal? Uh-oh.
There's a mysterious case of smuggled snakes.
It's Tom and Sophie to the rescue!

OUT NOW

More amazing behind-the-scenes animal action
at London Zoo
with the Nightingale family!

Run! The Elephant Weighs a Ton!
by Adam Frost

The animal-mad Nightingale family are charging out
of town towards a jumbo-sized mystery. Their animal
friends need them. Whoa! What a fright for the new baby
elephant. Something just isn't right. It's up to Tom and
Sophie to find out what!

OUT NOW

Don't miss exciting adventures
in the realm of the Amur tiger in

Paw Prints in the Snow
by Sally Grindley

Joe and his family are in Russia on the trail of one of the
world's rarest creatures, the beautiful Amur tiger.

Exploring a vast, freezing nature reserve, Joe comes closer
to the tigers than he ever imagined – and is drawn into a
daring mission to rescue an injured cub . . .

OUT NOW